chicken cheeks

chicken cheeks

(the beginning of the ends)

Michael Ian Black

Kevin Hawkes

SIMON & SCHUSTER BOOKS FOR YOUNG READERS
An imprint of Simon & Schuster Children's Publishing Division • 1230 Avenue of the Americas, New York, New York 10020 • Book design by Dan Potash • The text for this book is set in Caslon Antique. • The illustrations for this book are rendered in acrylics. • Manufactured in China • 6 8 10 9 7 5
Library of Congress Cataloging-in-Publication Data • Black, Michael Ian. • Chicken cheeks / Michael Ian Black; illustrated by Kevin Hawkes.—1st ed. • p. cm. • Summary: Illustrations and simple text describe the back ends of various animals. ISBN: 978-1-4169-4864-3 (hardcover) [1. Buttocks—Fiction. 2. Anatomy—Fiction. 3. Animals—Fiction. 4. Stories in rhyme.] I. Hawkes, Kevin, ill. II. Title. PZ8.3.B52915Chi 2008 [E]—dc22 2007016872 0914 SCP

For Elijah and Ruth, who laugh in all the right places
—M. I. B.

To all the sharks in the Perkes clan
—K. H.

Simon & Schuster Books for Young Readers
New York London Toronto Sydney

Duck tail

Moose caboose

Chicken cheeks

Penguin patootie

Polar bear derriere

Turkey tushy

Gnu wazoo

Flamingo fanny

Rhinoceros rump

Giraffe back half

Hound dog heinie

Toucan can

Kangaroo keister

Guinea pig buns

Deer rear

Duck-billed platypus
gluteus maximus

Bumblebee
bum!

The

ends